Y0-EGG-816

THINGS THAT GO

STICKER ACTIVITY BOOK

Pull out the sticker sheets and keep
them by you as you complete each page.
There are also lots of extra stickers to
use in this book or anywhere you want!
Have fun!

NATIONAL GEOGRAPHIC
Washington, D.C.

Editorial, Design, and Production by
make believe ideas

Picture credits: All images Shutterstock unless noted as follows: 1000 Words/Shutterstock.com: 33mc (UK police car); 2p2play/Shutterstock.com: 14tr (Hong Kong transportation); Baloncici/Shutterstock.com: 13bl (Eurostar train); Bob Pool/Shutterstock.com: 4tr (cowboy with herd); BrandonKleinVideo/Shutterstock.com: 33mtl (NYPD police car); Checubus/Shutterstock.com: 33tr (police motorcycle); dcdebs/iStock/Getty Images: 3l (boy on roller skates); Gagliardilmages/Shutterstock.com: 15b (London Tube train); jan kranendonk/Shutterstock.com: 37tl (motorcycle); Make Believe Ideas: 2bcl (clownfish), 2bcr (yellow fish), 2bl (fish), 2br (blue fish), 2mbl (starfish, seashell), 9br (ThrustSSC), 18tr/br (blue balloon x2), 26m/27l (clownfish x5), 27mr (ray), 28tl (digger), 28tr (dump truck), 29br (hay bale), 30tl (log truck), 30tr (cement truck), 31b (dirt background), 31tl (black car), 32tr (police car), 33br (policeman on horse), 36tc (ambulance); nalyvme/Shutterstock.com: 34tl (aerial platform); Patrick Wang/Shutterstock.com: 19mc (sea rescue helicopter); PhotoStock10/Shutterstock.com: 17tr (red-yellow-blue stunt plane); real444/iStock/Getty Images: 23bl (child with telescope); roibu/Shutterstock.com: 6tr (car production line); Vladimir Arndt/Shutterstock.com: 20l (Vostok 1); Wayne0216/Shutterstock.com: 1ml (bullet train).

Sticker pages: All images Shutterstock unless noted as follows: A. Aleksandravicius/Shutterstock.com: sticker page 2bc (inside a subway car); Alex JW Robinson/Shutterstock.com: sticker page 3mtr (emergency helicopter); Andrei Kobylko/Shutterstock.com: sticker page 3tr (fire helicopter); Art Konovalov/Shutterstock.com: sticker page 5mc (off-road truck); BrandonKleinVideo/Shutterstock.com: sticker page 5tc (NYPD police car); Checubus/Shutterstock.com: sticker page 5tr (police motorcycle); Darq/Shutterstock.com: sticker page 6mtl (sports car); FloridaStock/Shutterstock.com: sticker page 2mtr (steam train); Gestur Gislason/Shutterstock.com: sticker page 3mtc (TV news helicopter); LagunaticPhoto/Shutterstock.com: sticker page 2tl (Dodge Tomahawk); Make Believe Ideas: sticker page 1tmc (bike), sticker page 2 extra stickers (air balloon 2 x3), sticker page 3tc (blue balloon), sticker page 3mc (yellow car), sticker page 4tr (Jet Ski), sticker page 4bc (yellow car), sticker page 4br (blue car), sticker page 8 extra stickers (green bike x2, yellow car, blue car, red digger, red tractor x3, yellow lorry x2, sailboat x2, yellow car front, blue quadbike, blue tractor, red truck, red helicopter, green truck); Nildo Scoop/Shutterstock.com: sticker page 1bl (superkart); public domain image: sticker page 1br (Benz Patent Motor Car); Wayne0216/Shutterstock.com: sticker page 2mc (bullet train).

Make Believe Ideas would like to thank the Coventry Transport Museum for its support and assistance.

Printed in China. 19/MBI/1

There are lots of things that go!

People can travel on land, across the ocean, and through the air with things that go!

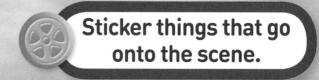 Sticker things that go onto the scene.

airplane

helicopter

car

train

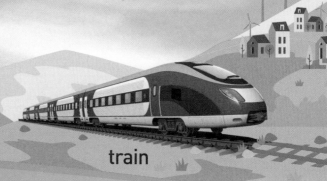

Color the large cruise ship.

cruise ship

2

digger

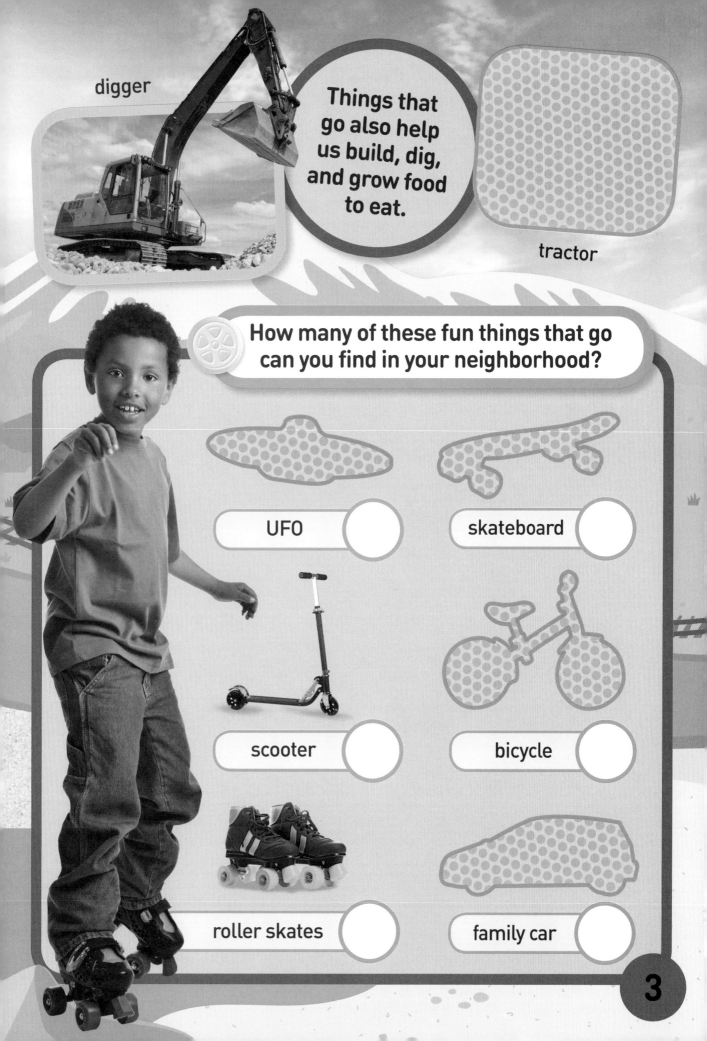

Things that go also help us build, dig, and grow food to eat.

tractor

How many of these fun things that go can you find in your neighborhood?

UFO

skateboard

scooter

bicycle

roller skates

family car

We've been on the move for a long time!

Before cars, tractors, and trains, we used animals to move around, farm the land, and carry heavy things.

a cowboy riding a horse

🧲 Sticker the animals that helped people travel.

camel

elephant

horse

The wheel helped us move and led to lots of other cool inventions.

Around 1478, the artist Leonardo da Vinci designed one of the first cars!

Leonardo da Vinci

Design your own car in the space below.

Sticker its wheels!

What will your car carry?

☐ people   ☐ food   ☐ animals   ☐ heavy things

Around **140 cars** are made every minute!

Cars are built piece by piece by workers and machines on production lines in factories around the world.

a car production line

 Help build the car on the production line.

1. car body made

2. body painted

4. car assembled

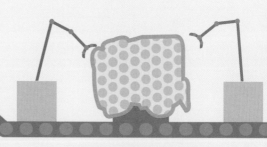

3. engine built

5. doors and wheels fitted

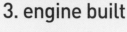
6. ready for a test drive

The United States has the most connecting roads in the world!

Find and count the cars on the road.

VROOM! How fast can cars go?

The first cars could only drive 10 miles per hour (16 km/h), which is about the same as a person running fast!

Benz Patent Motor Car

Add the numbers below to see who wins the race.

2 + 4 = _____

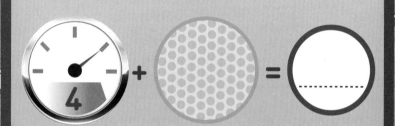
4 + = _____

+ 3 = _____

A speedometer tells the driver how fast he or she is driving.

8

Color this superfast car!

Match the cars to their top speeds.

240
mph
(386 km/h)

140
mph
(225 km/h)

150
mph
(241 km/h)

race car

superkart

family car

The ThrustSSC is the fastest car ever. Its top speed is faster than a flying jumbo jet!

9

People can also move on **two wheels!**

The dandy horse was an early type of bike and it worked a lot like a modern balance bike.

balance bike

 Sticker the missing bikes, then match the pairs.

bicycle

penny-farthing

tricycle

tandem

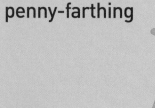

Motorcycles have an engine like a car and can drive really, really fast. Some can reach speeds of up to 350 miles per hour (563 km/h)!

Dodge Tomahawk motorcycle

Full steam ahead!

One of the first motorcycles was powered by steam!

Roper steam velocipede

Use the grid to draw the motorcycle.

Trains move over land on railroad tracks.

Trains were invented more than 200 years ago and helped move things, such as wood, coal, and iron.

Stephenson's Rocket

 Sticker the types of trains.

diesel train

steam train

bullet train

maglev train

electric train

Modern trains use diesel fuel, electricity, and even magnets to move.

Complete the railroad tracks.

PARIS

The Eurostar train travels under the English Channel through a big tunnel that connects London with Paris.

13

How do you travel around town?

There are lots of different ways to travel around big cities, including buses, trolleys, and taxis.

city transportation in Hong Kong

Find the different types of public transportation in the word search.

bus
cable car
monorail
subway
taxi
trolley

m	o	n	o	r	a	i	l
a	r	w	c	e	e	z	w
t	y	z	a	c	t	p	i
g	x	s	b	f	n	f	s
t	r	o	l	l	e	y	u
q	w	k	e	b	i	e	b
b	u	s	c	o	h	p	w
g	j	t	a	x	i	x	a
a	y	f	r	y	v	z	y

school bus

Many cities have underground stations and train tracks that run through deep tunnels.

inside a subway car

Park

Museum

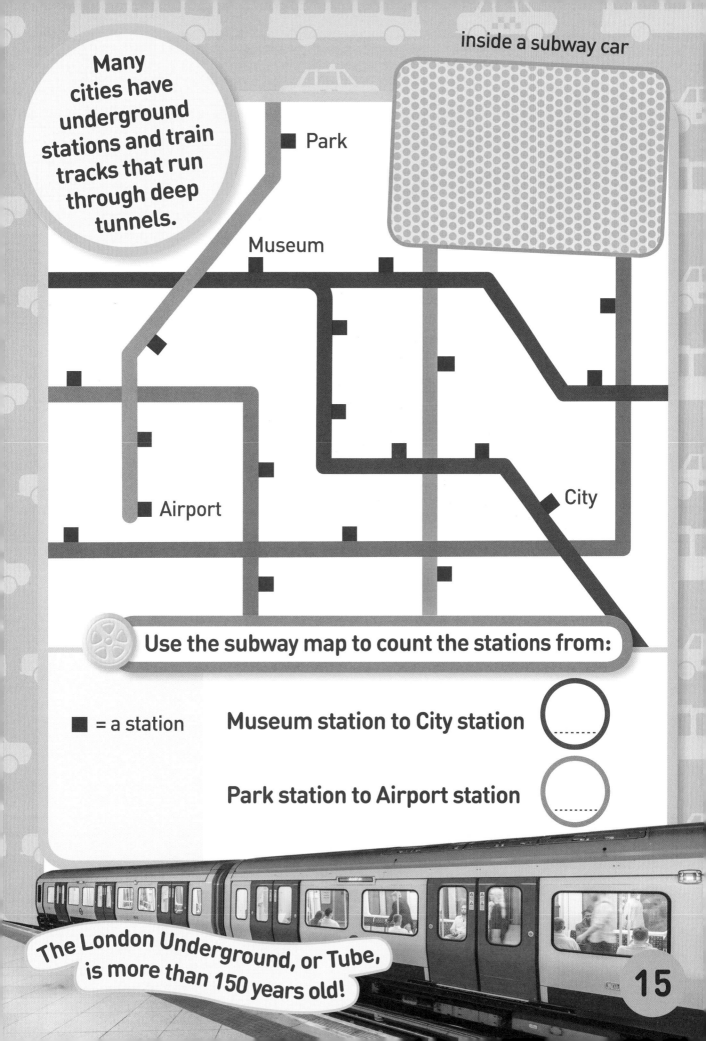

Airport

City

Use the subway map to count the stations from:

■ = a station

Museum station to City station (..........)

Park station to Airport station (..........)

The London Underground, or Tube, is more than 150 years old!

Planes soar through the sky!

Planes fly high in the sky and can be really big, carrying hundreds of people, or really small with just a pilot.

seaplane

Match the high-flying things to their shadows.

jumbo jet

hang glider

biplane

16

Trace the flight paths of these colorful stunt planes.

Watch me do a loop!

In 1903, the Wright brothers piloted the first airplane. The flight only lasted for 12 seconds!

Orville Wright

Wilbur Wright

Connect the dots to see the plane the Wright brothers flew.

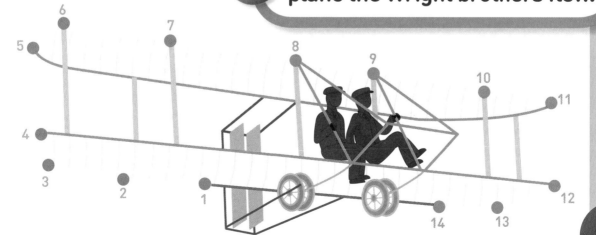

There are other ways to **fly** in the **sky!**

Before airplanes, the only way to fly was to float upward in crafts like hot-air balloons.

Can you spot and circle this balloon in the sky?

1 2 3 4

3
2
1
2
1
2
3
4
3
2
3
2

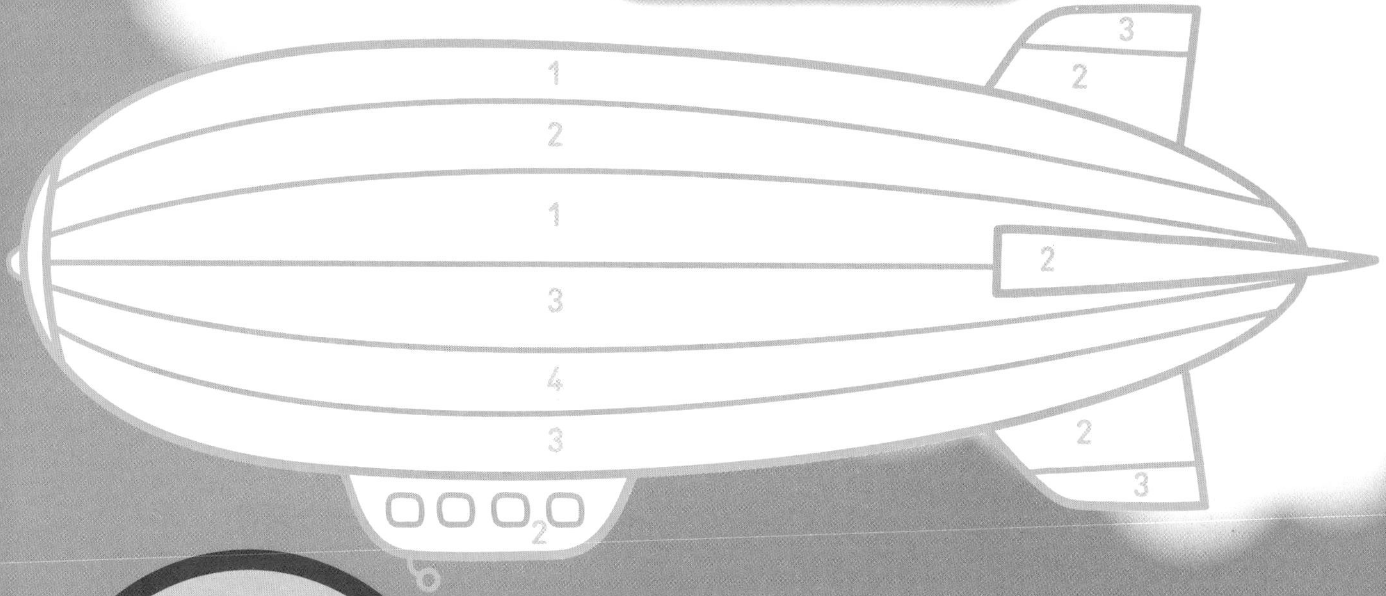

Helicopters use a propeller to fly. They can lift off the ground and hover in the air.

Sticker the different jobs that helicopters are used for.

sea rescue

firefighting

TV news

emergency help

19

Spacecraft blast off into outer space!

Spacecraft are made by scientists and use computers and powerful engines to fly into space.

space shuttle

If you were going to space, what would your spaceship look like?

Vostok 1

Vostok 1 was the first spacecraft to launch an astronaut into space!

Stickers for pages 2 and 3

Stickers for pages 4 and 5

Stickers for pages 6 and 7

Stickers for pages 8 and 9

Stickers for pages 10 and 11

Stickers for pages 12 and 13

LONDON

Extra stickers

Stickers for pages 14 and 15

SCHOOL BUS

Stickers for pages 16 and 17

Stickers for pages 18 and 19

Stickers for pages 22 and 23

Stickers for page 21

Stickers for pages 24 and 25

Stickers for pages 26 and 27

Stickers for pages 28 and 29

Stickers for pages 30 and 31

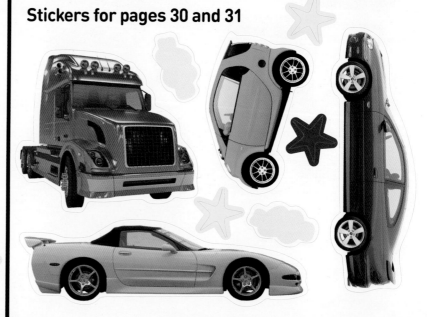

Stickers for pages 32 and 33

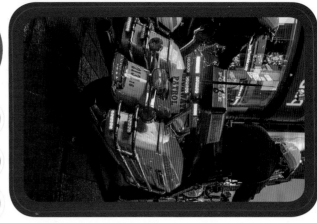

Stickers for pages 34 and 35

Stickers for pages 36 and 37

14 NGK

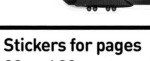

Stickers for pages 38 and 39

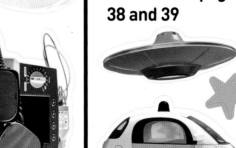

Stickers for page 40

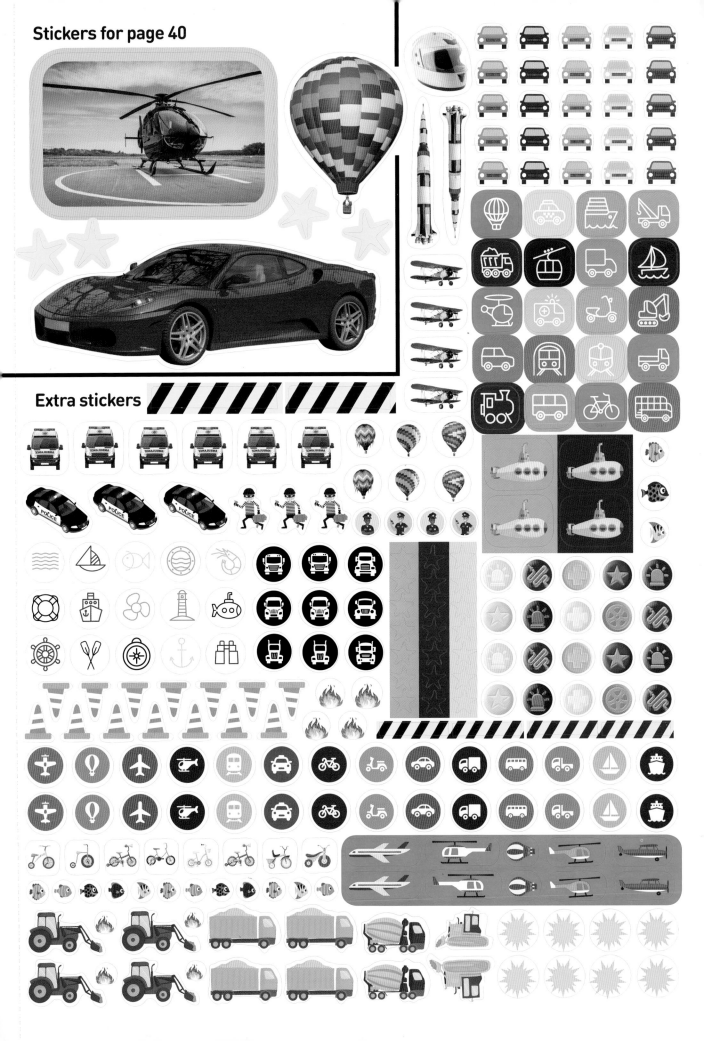

Extra stickers

Extra stickers

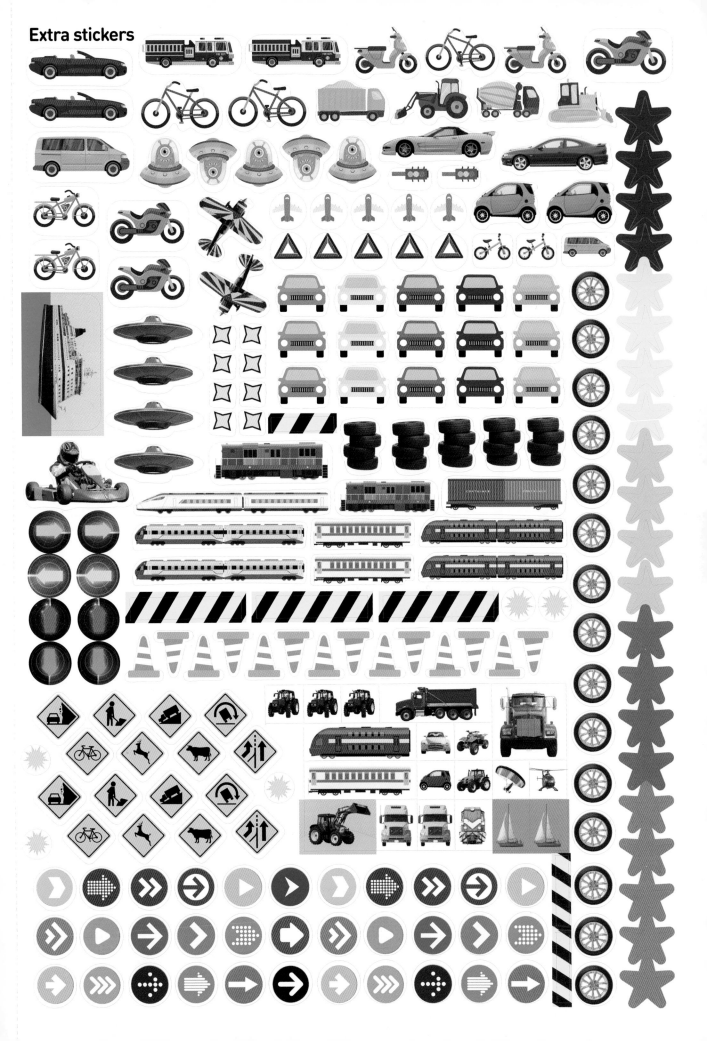

Extra stickers

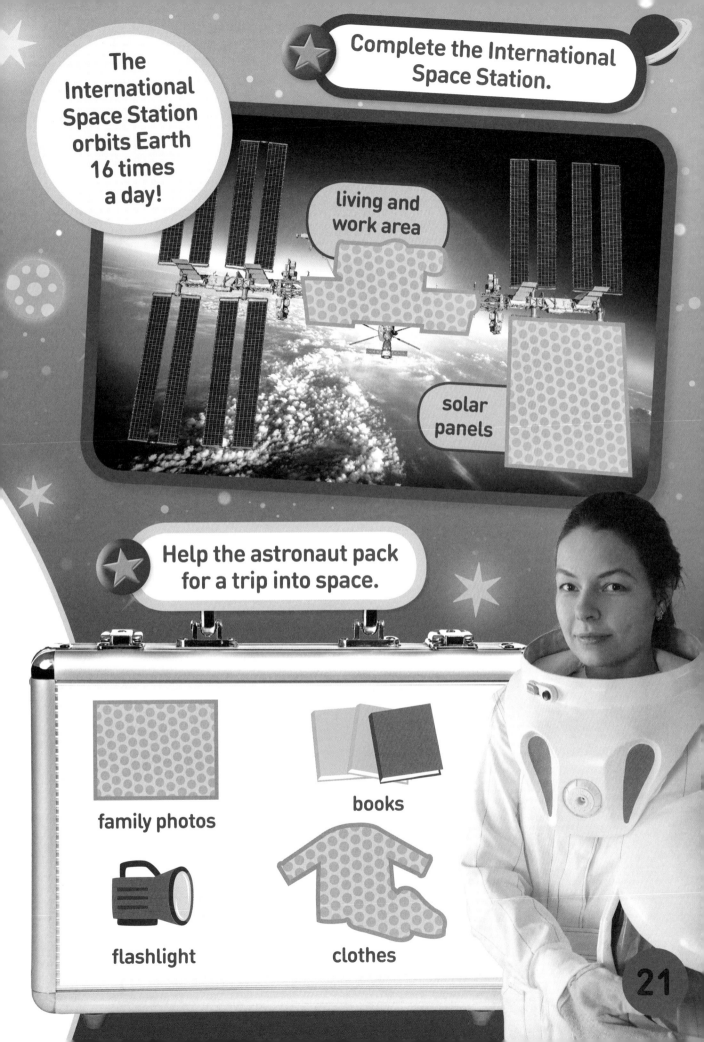

Land ahoy! Ships sail across the sea.

Modern ships use big engines to sail thousands of miles around the world.

cargo ship

fishing trawler

tanker

Sticker the things each ship is carrying.

Long ago, ships were the only way to travel across the oceans and explore the world.

Which island is the explorer Vasco da Gama sailing to?

I'm looking for an island with a volcano and two trees.

What's sailing on the horizon?

Viking longship

23

Some boats are small, fast, and strong!

Complete the jigsaws to see what each tugboat is pulling.

Tugboats are small but very strong! They push and pull bigger boats and ships in and out of busy ports.

Army tugboats are so strong they can pull a giant aircraft carrier!

Speedboats and Jet Skis are lots of fun on the water. They zoom over the waves at superfast speeds!

Which speedboat is pulling the water-skier?

sailboat

water-skier

Jet Ski

speedboat

speedboat

A hovercraft travels across water and land on an air cushion.

Color in the hovercraft.

25

Submarines explore deep underwater!

Submarines can travel deep underwater. We use them to study life below the waves.

Use the codebreaker to see how deep underwater each location is.

		⚓					🐟		
0	**1**	**2**	**3**	**4**	**5**	**6**	**7**	**8**	**9**

shipwreck

.... fathoms

coral reef

.... fathoms

26 A fathom is about the same as the height of one horse.

Submarines use a special machine called sonar to help them see in the dark, murky seas.

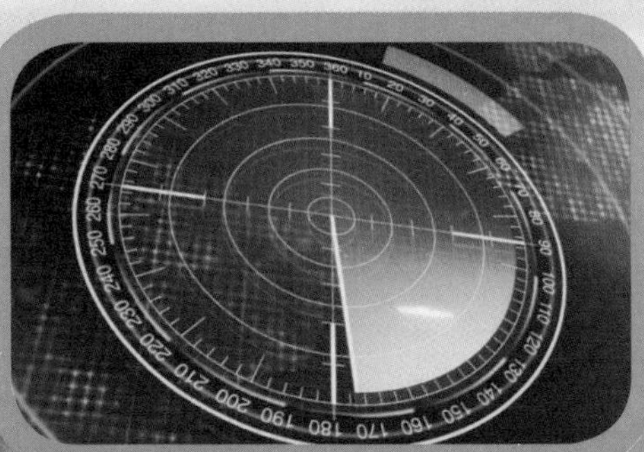

sonar display

finish

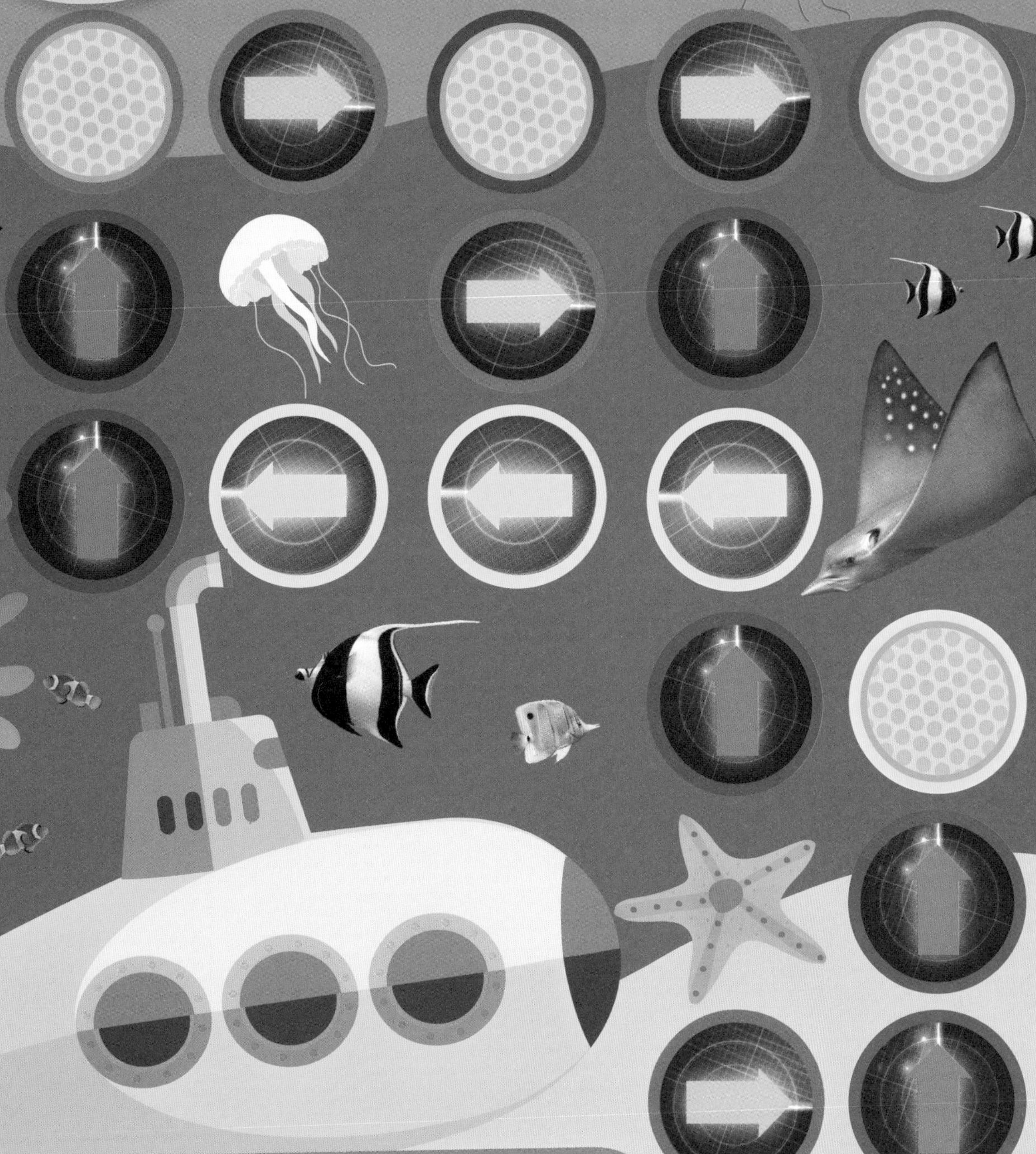

start

Guide the submarine through the coral reef back to the surface.

Some vehicles help us **build,** dig, and plow.

digger

We use things that go to help us build tall buildings, dig deep holes, and lift heavy loads.

dump truck

Sticker the things that go on the construction site.

digger

cement mixer

dump truck

bulldozer

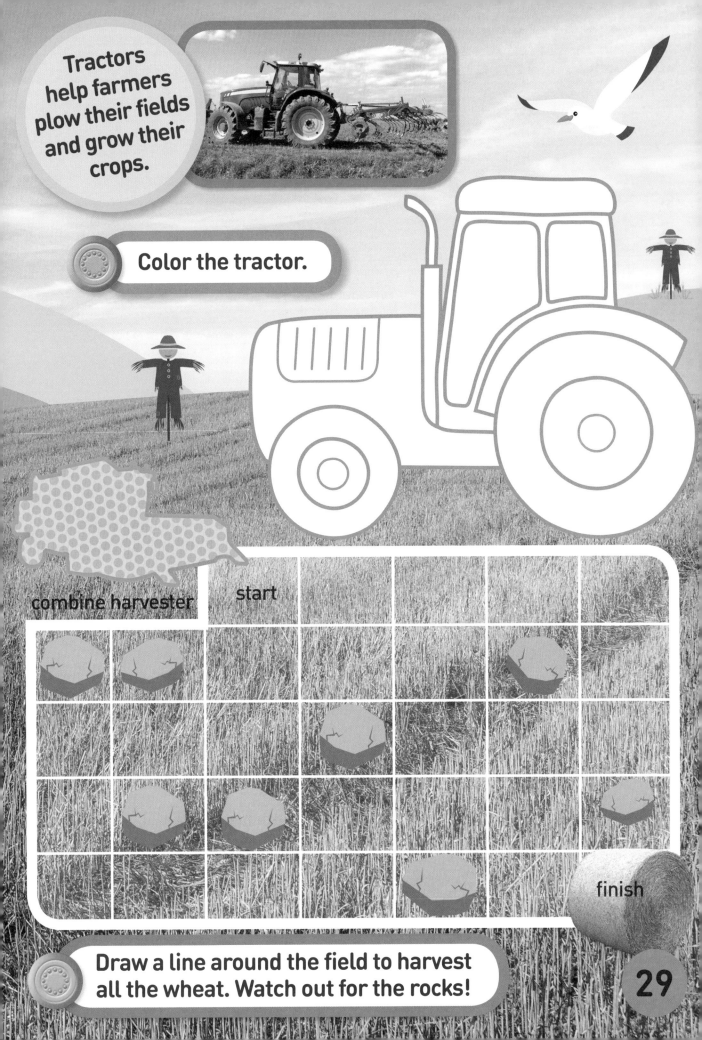

Tractors help farmers plow their fields and grow their crops.

Color the tractor.

combine harvester

start

finish

Draw a line around the field to harvest all the wheat. Watch out for the rocks!

29

Trucks have big engines and big wheels!

Trucks can pull trailers with heavy loads. Some trucks carry machinery, animals, and even logs!

cement truck

garbage truck

 Which cargo does the truck need to collect?

Clues:

The cargo canister is blue.

The canister has a stripe on it.

The cargo boxes are brown.

The cargo is a food.

Sticker the cars on the transporter.

Monster trucks have giant wheels that are about as tall as an adult!

Color the monster truck using the key.

1 2 3 4 5

The police use vehicles to keep us safe!

Police officers use bikes, cars, motorcycles, and horses to make sure they are first to the scene!

police car

police motorcycle

 Guide the police car back to the police station and pick up the five bank robbers along the way.

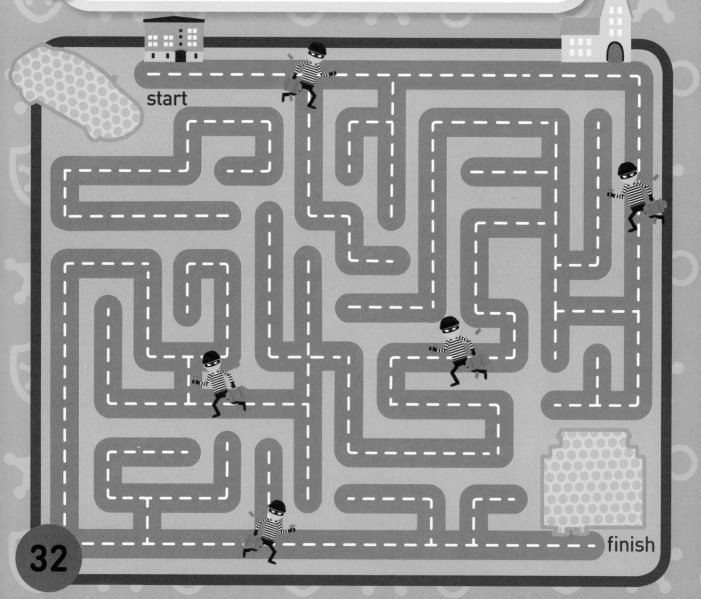

start

finish

Police sirens are bright, loud, and rumble so people can see, hear, and feel the police coming.

Match the close-up sirens to the police vehicles.

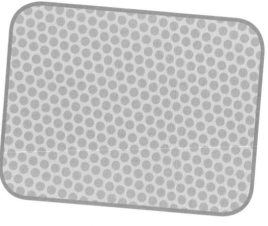

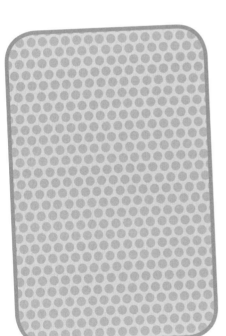

Did you know that people are more likely to talk to a police officer when he or she is on a police horse?

Fire vehicles can put out any fire!

Firefighters have different vehicles for every type of emergency. They can save the day anywhere—any time!

off-road fire truck

A fire truck holds up to 1,000 gallons (3,785 L) of water. That's the same as 11,000 cans of soda!

Which hose is connected to the fire truck and is ready to use?

Sticker the fire truck, then spot the five differences.

Fire planes drop water and chemicals to stop wildfires.

Can you find all the fire equipment from a fire truck in the word search?

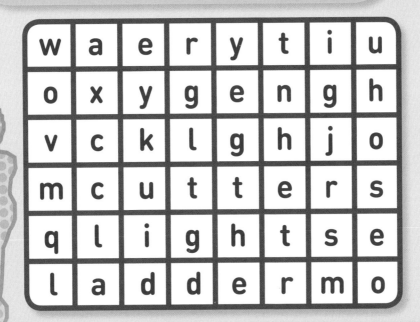

w	a	e	r	y	t	i	u
o	x	y	g	e	n	g	h
v	c	k	l	g	h	j	o
m	c	u	t	t	e	r	s
q	l	i	g	h	t	s	e
l	a	d	d	e	r	m	o

ax

cutters

hose

ladder

lights

oxygen

35

Ambulances speed to people in need!

An ambulance is like a mini hospital on wheels, and has everything paramedics need to treat patients on the go!

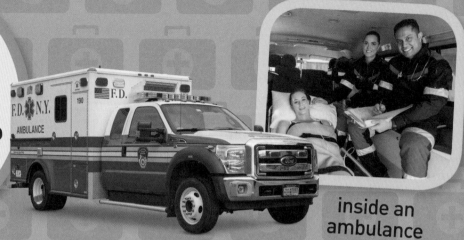

inside an ambulance

Guide the ambulance to the patient by passing the cars with even numbers in their license plates.

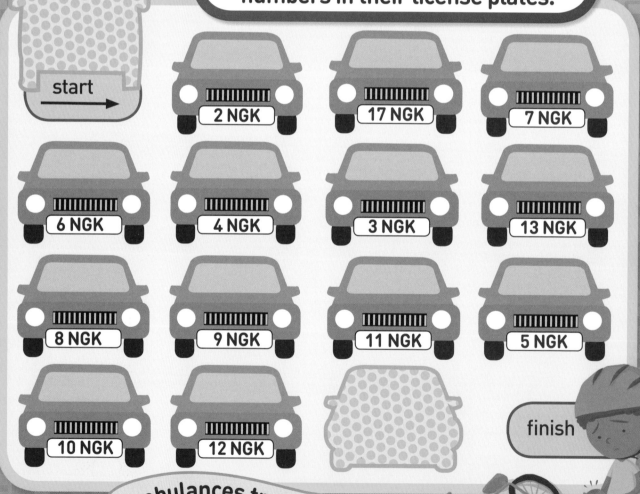

start

2 NGK   17 NGK   7 NGK

6 NGK   4 NGK   3 NGK   13 NGK

8 NGK   9 NGK   11 NGK   5 NGK

10 NGK   12 NGK   finish

Ambulances try to get to patients within eight minutes!

Medics use motorcycles to drive through busy traffic.

Sticker the equipment for the motorcycling medic.

helmet

GPS

compact defibrillator

In Australia, the Royal Flying Doctor Service uses planes to reach patients who live far from towns and cities.

medicine

Guide the Flying Doctor to the correct farmhouse.

start

Directions:

1. Move right 5

2. Move down 4

3. Move left 3

4. Move up 1

37

How will we **travel** in the **future?**

Our roads might be full of driverless cars! They will drive you around town using special tools and sensors.

⭐ Guide the driverless car around the obstacles.

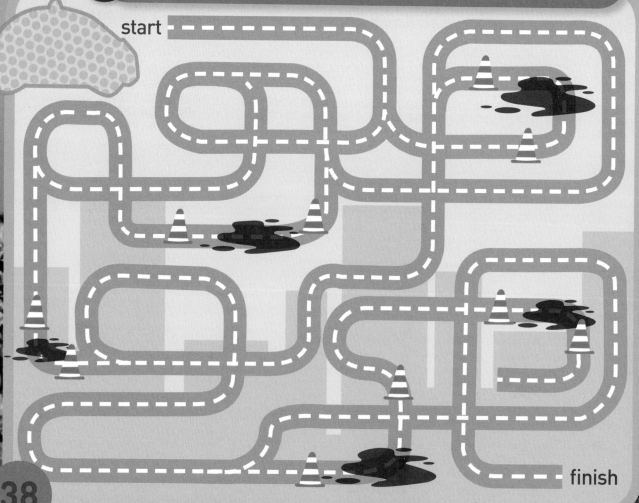

start

finish

SpaceX's Dragon spacecraft

Some companies are trying to be the first to fly tourists into space!

Color the spaceplane and moon hotel.

Time for a space-cation!

How many UFOs can you count? ....

What are your favorite things that go?

I love planes!

Find the missing stickers.

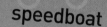
speedboat

helicopter

hot-air balloon

Draw your favorite things that go.

sports car